Mills & Bo
is pr

THE MAN SHE'LL MARRY

by best-selling author and reader favourite
Carole Mortimer

Welcome to this delightful romance where a man and a woman, both happily single, are hit by a thunderbolt—instant attraction!

Single mum Merry Baker long ago decided marriage wasn't on the cards for her. And when handsome wealthy Zack Kingston proposes after they've only just met, she thinks it has to be too good to be true. But should Merry follow her head…or her heart? Could it be that Zack really *is* the man she'll marry?

Read on to find out…

Carole Mortimer says 'I was born in England, the youngest of three children—I have two older brothers. I started writing in 1978, and have now written over 100 books for Mills & Boon®.

'I have four sons—Matthew, Joshua, Timothy and Peter—and a bearded collie dog called Merlyn. I'm in a very happy relationship with Peter senior; we're best friends as well as lovers, which is probably the best receipe for a successful relationship. We live on the Isle of Man.'

Look out for Carole Mortimer's next book in
Modern Romance™

The Secret Virgin
available September 2001!

PRAISE FOR THE AUTHOR

'Carole Mortimer dishes up outstanding reading as she blends dynamic characters, volatile scenes, superb chemistry and a wonderful premise.'
—*Romantic Times* on *Married by Christmas*

'...laughter, tears, suspense and winning romance.'
—*Romantic Times* on *Joined by Marriage*

'Readers should definately keep those tissues handy for this one.'
—*Romantic Times* on *Private Lives*

First published in Great Britain 1999
Harlequin Mills & Boon Limited,
Eton House, 18-24 Paradise Road, Richmond, Surrey, TW9 1SR
This edition 2001

ISBN 0 263 83168 X

54-0701

Printed and bound in Great Britain
by Bookmarque Ltd, Croydon, Surrey.

The Man She'll Marry

Carole Mortimer

MILLS & BOON®

CHAPTER ONE

'Is your mother at home?'

Merry stared at the man who stood on the doorstep. She knew she was being rude; her 'mother' had taught her all the necessary social niceties. But, looking the way this man did, he had to be used to women staring at him. Dani would have described him as 'drop-dead gorgeous', and for the first time Merry understood exactly what she meant by that phrase; this man had to set female hearts pounding, pulses racing, wherever he went!

'Is Dani anything like you?'

The second question was fired at her before she'd even had chance to formulate an answer to the first one. It had been a long day, and she had only got in a short time ago, though long enough to have quickly changed into an old pair of black denims Dani had outgrown some years before, and a sloppy green jumper that hung loosely down to mid-thigh. Not exactly the height of fashion, but she was comfortable.

At least she had been, until faced with the elegance of her visitor. This man, well over six feet in height, with his 'drop-dead gorgeous' good looks—slightly overlong blond hair, a face that looked hewn from granite, eyes a deep blue, nose long and arrogant, mouth sensual above a squarely challenging jaw—wore his own designer-label clothes with a complete disregard for those labels, or for how well his blue jacket and pale blue shirt emphasised the width of his shoulders and the narrowness of his waist, his blue jeans simply adding to his rugged handsomeness. Dani's cast-offs, which were slightly too big at that, did not do the same for her own appearance!

He frowned at her now, although the laughter lines beside his eyes and mouth said he wasn't always this serious. '*Is* your mother at home?' he persisted.

'No,' she answered him honestly, intrigued in spite of herself. Oh, not by his looks; good looks alone had never impressed her. Well, only the once. And she had learnt bitterly from the experience. No, what intrigued her about this particular man was that he obviously knew of Dani but he had no idea what Dani actually looked like…!

Because Dani was nothing like Merry. Her own long hair was dark, almost black, whereas Dani's was a riot of blonde curls, and Dani's eyes were brown, whereas her own were green, and Dani, at eighteen, was much taller than her own five foot nothing. So who was this man? He knew *of* Dani, but nothing else about her—except her address…

He gave an impatient sigh. 'I don't suppose your sister is here, either? No.' He answered his own question. 'David said they were going to some coffee shop or other this evening. Damn,' he muttered, looking thoughtful. 'I don't suppose I could come in and wait, could I?' His imperious tone of voice totally belied the request that his words should have been.

A man used to getting his own way, Merry surmised ruefully. Probably in his late thirties, and with no ring on his left hand to say whether or not he was married. The fact that he wasn't wearing a ring said he would do as he damn well pleased, not that he wasn't actually *married*. Everything about this man quietly cried self-assurance and determination.

'No, I don't suppose you could,' she answered dryly.

Blond brows rose over those deep blue eyes, his mouth quirking wryly. 'Well, at least one of the family seems to have some sense!' he allowed.

She remembered again that it had been a long day and she had only been home from work for a short time; what she really wanted right now was to sit down with a glass of cooled white wine and simply unwind before thinking about preparing dinner. Her unexpected guest did not fit in with those plans at all. Besides, exactly what did he want to come in and wait *for*?

'One of the family?' she echoed smoothly, the mildness of her tone totally masking her impatience.

He nodded. 'You and Dani. You are obviously the elder—'

'Obviously,' she acknowledged crisply. Why state the *obvious*?

He gave her a sharp look, visibly making an effort to relax. 'I didn't mean to sound insulting, Miss Baker—'

'You may not have meant to, Mr…?' She paused pointedly; he knew her name while she had absolutely no idea what his might be.

'Kingston,' he supplied. 'Zack Kingston.'

Merry frowned. Kingston? The name *did* sound familiar. Dani had mentioned someone at university by that name. David Kingston… 'David would be your son—'

'Nephew,' Zack Kingston corrected. 'Dani has obviously talked to you about him!'

Merry didn't like the accusation in his tone. Any more than she liked standing on the doorstep having this conversation with him. 'Mr Kingston, I was just about to have a glass of wine. Would you like to join me?' Green eyes steadily met blue.

How much 'sense' did he think she had now? The trouble with Mr Zack Kingston was that he formed snap judgements, and had taken one look at her and decided she was small and defenceless. It was only one of several wrong assumptions he had made!

That direct blue gaze was reassessing now, moving slowly from her bare feet, over the faded black denims, the too-large jumper, to the wild cascade of her long dark hair, the small gamine face dominated by challenging eyes.

To Merry's amusement, she could see he was none the wiser for his review of her. She obviously didn't look to him what she actually was. There was something to be said for a man-free—and therefore problem-free—life, after all!

'Make your mind up, Mr Kingston,' she advised mockingly. 'I don't intend standing here all evening waiting for your answer!'

Anger flared briefly in his deep blue eyes before he quickly brought it under control. Here was a man used to calling the shots, Merry guessed again, not the other way around. Well, this was her home, and her time, and if he wanted to continue this conversation he could do it inside, where she could relax. She had absolutely no idea what he was doing here, what it had to do with Dani—if anything—and she had no intention of discussing it any further standing on the doorstep!

'You'll be quite safe, Mr Kingston,' she added derisively. 'I make it a rule never to attack defenceless men on—what is it today?—on a Tuesday evening,' she teased as she turned and walked back inside the house, sure he would follow her; he had come here this evening with something to say, and unless she was mistaken he hadn't said it yet!

'I can assure you, Miss Baker, I am far from defenceless!'

She was right; he *had* followed her! And as she looked up from pouring two glasses of wine she tried hard not to notice how his large frame dominated the bright but compact kitchen. 'You are?' she returned as she handed him his glass.

'I are— I mean— Oh, hell.' He scowled. 'Tell me, Miss Baker—'

'Merry,' she put in lightly, sitting up on one of the bar stools. 'Short for Meredith,' she tacked on, to save him the bother of asking; he was the sort of man who would want to know!

He nodded. 'Tell me, Merry,' he murmured softly as he sat on the second bar stool, his bent knee only inches away from her own. 'What happens to ''defenceless men'' on the other evenings of the week?'

Different approach. Anger hadn't worked, so now

he was going to try cajoling, revealing some of that humour she had guessed at when she first saw him.

Merry quirked dark brows at him over the top of her wine glass. 'Why don't you come back tomorrow and find out?' she replied.

For a moment he looked perplexed. And then he smiled, and laughed.

Whew! Merry continued sipping her wine, mainly as a way of hiding the way her breath had caught in her throat. 'Drop-dead gorgeous'! That laugh only made him more so. A young Robert Redford, she decided admiringly.

He sobered, shaking his head as he still smiled. 'If Dani is anything like you, then I think I understand David's dilemma,' he said.

'David has a dilemma?' she prompted softly.

The laughter had all gone now; Zack Kingston's expression one of grim disapproval. '*I* consider it a dilemma, but I doubt that he does!'

Merry didn't understand how his nephew's dilemma could have anything to do with Dani. Dani had begun her studies at university at the end of September, and, being gregarious by nature, she had quickly made friends. David Kingston was only one of several Dani had mentioned during the last couple of months. Merry certainly couldn't think of any reason for the boy's uncle to come here in search of Dani...

'When do you expect your mother home?' Zack Kingston continued restlessly, putting down his glass of barely touched white wine.

Which wasn't altogether fair on the wine. Merry

didn't consider herself a connoisseur by any means, but her taste was discerning, and the wine was a delicious Chablis, perfectly chilled.

'I don't,' she told him consideringly. 'David's dilemma has something to do with Dani?' An uneasy fluttering sensation was beginning in the pit of her stomach.

Dani wasn't only gregarious, she was absolutely beautiful. And there was no bias involved in that observation; Dani had been bowling men off their feet since she was in her cradle!

'Tell me,' Merry said slowly, 'is David anything like you?'

'What the hell does that have to do—?' Zack Kingston broke off, shaking his head impatiently. 'David was the son of my older brother and his wife. Unfortunately they were both killed in a car accident ten years ago, which is when I took over his guardianship.'

Very commendable, considering the demands a child could make on you—even more so when he wasn't actually your own…

'That doesn't actually answer my question, Mr Kingston,' Merry persisted.

'I don't see what it has to do with anything—'

'It has a great deal to do with it,' she said tersely; a twenty-ish version of this man could be devastating to a girl like Dani. 'David is tall, blond, and gorgeous, right?'

Now he was the one to look mockingly at her. 'Like me?' he returned.

Merry glared at him. 'You're too old to be playing these sort of games, Mr Kingston—'

'The name is Zack—Merry,' he cut in. 'And I don't consider myself ''too old'' for anything!'

The chill in his tone would have frozen a lesser woman into silence, but Merry didn't consider herself a 'lesser' anything! And she never would!

'So David *is* like you?' she said irritably. Oh, Dani, sweet Dani, what have you done?

Zack shrugged. 'There's a certain similarity, yes. But—'

'It's enough,' Merry waved a dismissive hand. 'Dani told me she was meeting friends for coffee this evening. Am I to take it David is that friend?' Singular, not plural. But not exactly a lie, either. Not that she had thought for a moment that it would be; she and Dani had never lied to each other.

Those blue eyes were narrowed now. 'That's what he told me before he left this morning to attend classes, yes,' Zack agreed. 'Amongst other things,' he added. 'I called here earlier in the day in the hope I could talk to Dani's mother without—'

'I work, Mr Kingston,' Merry told him caustically. Unlike some people, obviously… The cut of his clothes, and that air of arrogance, spoke of wealth, and a nature that didn't suffer fools gladly. Well, she certainly didn't have the former, but she didn't suffer fools, either; and this man was taking an awful long time to get to his point!

He was staring at her now, seemingly speechless—not something that happened often, Merry was sure!

She had realised a few minutes ago that he assumed she was Dani's sister.

'I suggest we dispense with any misconceptions you may have formed when you arrived, Mr Kingston,' she told him briskly. 'Dani doesn't *have* a sister, older or otherwise. In fact, Dani is an only child.' She met his eyes steadily.

Zack Kingston blinked, and then blinked again, his head tilted to one side as he reassessed the situation a second time. Finally he shook his head. 'You aren't old enough to be Dani's mother! Unless—' His gaze sharpened in dismay. 'Exactly how old is Dani?'

Merry was unabashed. 'Daniella—Dani—is eighteen.'

He looked relieved to hear that, but his puzzled vision returned to Merry once again, raking over her appearance once more, from the top of her head down to her bare toes, returning to her face—a face full of good humour, her green eyes clear and bright, her nose small and pert, her mouth wide and inclined to turn up at the corners, giving her a happy look even when she didn't feel much like smiling.

As she didn't now. This man, she had come to realise over the last few minutes, had come here to tell her something important about his nephew and her daughter. And in view of the way Dani had made her own way into life, Merry couldn't help the feelings of foreboding that were seething over her. She no longer found this man's mistake over her identity a cause for amusement, merely questioned the urgency of his need to talk to Dani's mother.

Zack drew in a controlling breath. 'Miss Baker— Er, Mrs—'

'*Miss* Baker,' Merry corrected stiltedly. What was that saying about 'the sins of the father'...? Did it also apply to 'the mistakes of the mother'? 'I've never been a Mrs Anything, Mr Kingston,' she informed him flatly, pointed chin raised defiantly.

He nodded abruptly. 'Well, Miss Baker, it appears you're about to have a wedding in the family now! My nephew David informed me this morning that he intends marrying your daughter!'

Merry swallowed hard, feeling the colour drain from her cheeks. Dani. Eighteen-year-old Dani. Beautiful Dani, who had her whole life before her. Dani, who had only been at university for two months. It couldn't be happening all over again!

Was the mistake of the mother being repeated by the daughter...?

CHAPTER TWO

'HERE, drink this,'

Merry looked up at Zack. 'This' turned out to be what was left of the wine in his glass. There could only be one reason—in the present circumstances!—why Zack Kingston was encouraging her to drink it.

She pushed the glass away, glaring at him. 'I am not in need of restorative alcohol, thank you,' she told him frostily. 'Did you say you have been David's guardian for the last ten years?'

'Almost ten and a half, to be exact,' he confirmed, frowning at the question.

Merry couldn't see what difference that six months made! 'Oh, let's, by all means, be exact,' she snapped caustically, looking him up and down, once again noticing the expensive cut of his clothes, his only jewellery a signet ring on the little finger of his right hand. 'Are you married, Mr Kingston?' she demanded in clipped tones.

His mouth twisted. 'Fortunately not.'

She had thought not; he didn't give the impression of a man in a hurry to get back to his home. Or a wife. 'You do have some intelligence, then,' she replied dismissively. 'In that case—'

'You consider it intelligent not to be married, Miss—Merry?' he interrupted.

She looked at him pityingly. She could well understand his amazement at finding a woman who wasn't interested in marriage; considering the way he looked, his apparent wealth and his bachelor status, she could imagine he had met far too many women desperate to get married—to him!

'As I've already pointed out to you, marriage is an unknown quantity to me personally.' She shrugged. 'And it seems to me, from the amount of separation and divorce, that marriage has become an overrated state to be in!'

'You—'

'However, that does not mean I advocate single motherhood, either,' she continued firmly. 'I know from experience how hard that can be. For the mother left on her own to bring up the child, not the father,' she added heatedly. 'He usually walks away without any responsibilities!'

That deep blue gaze watched her consideringly. 'Is that what happened to you?'

She bristled defensively. 'We weren't talking about me!' Merry snapped back.

Zack shook his head dazedly. 'Then I would like to know who we are talking about?'

'Dani, of course!' Despite her refusal of his wine a few minutes ago, she now took a grateful sip from her own glass. 'You are the boy's guardian. Didn't you teach him any of the facts of life?' She shook her head with angry disgust. 'Or are you one of those men who believe it's the woman's responsibility to take care of the precautions?' That seemed all too often to be the case nowadays; woman's demand for equality, and therefore independence, had rebounded on them in the case of sexual relationships!

'Dani suffers from a similar problem to me, in that she is medically unable to take the pill,' she told Zack coldly.

'I'll file that information away for future reference,' he said, sounding amused.

Merry could feel the heat in her cheeks. This man was making fun of her! 'I'm glad you find this situation funny, Mr Kingston—'

'"Funny" is far from the right word to describe how I feel about what's happened,' he bit out, suddenly looking at her with an arctic chill in his eyes. 'You are obviously under some misapprehension concerning Dani and David's relationship. Contrary to the conclusion you seem to have jumped to, your daughter is not pregnant!'

Merry stared at him uncomprehending. Not...? When Zack Kingston informed her of his nephew's determination to marry Dani, it had seemed to her there could be only one reason for such impetuosity. Distressing as that conclusion might have been. But he was saying Dani *wasn't* pregnant!

'I don't understand.' She shook her head.

'I *didn't*,' he rasped. 'But, having now met you, I'm beginning to!'

Merry looked at him blankly. What was that supposed to mean? What could she possibly have to do with his nephew's announcement that he intended marrying Dani; she had never even met the young man!

'Perhaps you would care to explain that remark?' she invited coolly, green eyes sparkling.

He gave an abrupt laugh. 'I most certainly would,' he rasped. 'You obviously have an attitude towards pre-marital sex—'

'I have an attitude towards marriage too!' she jumped in. How dared this man come into her home and make snap judgements about her? He didn't even know her! He was an arrogant swine, and if he thought she was going to let her daughter have anything to do with a relative of his, then he was sadly—

'We'll get to that in a minute,' he dismissed, with that arrogance she had just mentally attributed to him. 'I was about to say that, in the circumstances, your attitude towards pre-marital relationships is perfectly understandable.'

'Exactly what ''circumstances'' would you be referring to, Mr Kingston?' Merry prompted fiercely, raising herself to her full height of five feet and half an inch—and making absolutely no impression on him, judging by the way he looked down his arrogant nose at her!

As she had expected, he looked unperturbed. 'Obviously the circumstances of Dani's birth—'

'Which you know absolutely nothing about!' she returned furiously. He raised his blond brows questioningly. Well, he could question all he liked; it was none of his business what those 'circumstances' might have been! Besides, he seemed to have already drawn his own conclusions.

The silence stretched between them, as green eyes

warred with blue. But Merry had no intention of being the one to back down.

'Which I know absolutely nothing about,' Zack was finally the one to slowly admit. 'But I believe it has everything to do with Dani's own feelings towards relationships.'

'You already said that,' Merry retorted.

His mouth tightened. 'Having now thought about this, it's my belief—though I won't be able to confirm this until I've spoken to David again—that he and Dani are in love, and that, like all young people in love, they wish to consummate their physical attraction towards each other, but that Dani would rather wait until after they are married.'

'I can't see anything wrong with that,' Merry scorned.

'There is if their only solution to the problem is for them to marry immediately!' Zack returned exasperatedly.

Dani had watched Merry's struggles over the years to cope with working and being a mother, and she knew exactly how difficult it had been for Merry to acquire a career at all when she had become pregnant during her first term at university. *Had* that coloured Dani's own views on marriage and lovemaking? If it had, was that really such a bad thing? Dani was so young still, not much more than a child, really, not old enough for the responsibility of either marriage or a family.

Thinking of Dani dissipated Merry's anger and distress, cleared the initial panic from her mind. She and Dani were close, and she didn't believe, now that she could think straight, that Dani would agree to marry someone and then not tell her own mother about it. Admittedly, Dani seemed to have kept the intensity of this particular relationship with David Kingston to herself, not seeming to have mentioned him any more than the other new friends she had made in the last couple of months. But a marriage proposal, and its acceptance, was something else entirely…

Merry looked up at Zack Kingston with a new confidence. 'I don't believe they *have* decided to marry, immediately or otherwise,' she told him calmly. 'I think you may have been a little premature in coming here today, Mr Kingston—'

'For God's sake call me Zack!' he exploded. 'And no matter what you may think, Merry, I did not imagine David's announcement to me this morning—it totally destroyed my appetite for breakfast!'

Merry felt her mouth twitching with humour, had to bite her lip to stop herself from smiling. She could picture Zack now, seated at the end of a long dining table, newspaper spread out in front of him, while some meticulous, silent servant served him bacon and eggs—the latter would be scrambled, of course, no messy egg-yolks for this man to deal with! And then, just as he was about to take his first mouthful of the mouthwatering food, David dropping his bombshell!

'I trust you managed to eat lunch, Zack?' she said soothingly. 'It really isn't good for the blood sugar for you to go without food for too long. It impairs your judgement, and—'

'My judgement is not impaired, Merry,' he bit out. 'David told me—'

'I'm not disputing what he told you,' she assured him evenly. 'I'm merely questioning the validity of the news that *Dani* intends marrying *him*. I must admit I was thrown for a few minutes after your initial announcement, but I've had time to collect my thoughts now. I know Dani, the two of us are friends, as well as mother and daughter, and if she were serious about your nephew then I believe she would have told me about him.' Merry's confidence increased even as she spoke the words. She *did* know Dani, and what this man was suggesting didn't sound at all like her daughter. 'I don't disbelieve that David told you how he felt towards Dani—'

'Thank you for that, at least!' Zack snapped with sarcastic impatience.

She couldn't exactly blame him for feeling this way; he had obviously had a tough day since David's intentions had destroyed his breakfast. They had certainly dispelled her own earlier tiredness too!

'I don't mean to sound patronising, Zack,' she assured him. She might not have meant to, but in retrospect that was exactly what she had sounded! 'I'm just doubtful of Dani's part in all of this.' She absently poured them both another glassful of wine, wordlessly handing his over. 'Dani and I have never had secrets. There's never been any reason for us to,' she revealed, thinking of her own years without romantic involvement.

When Dani had been very young there just hadn't been the time, between studying and caring for a young child, and there had only been the occasional date in the years following. Most men of a similar age to herself were either already married, running away from an unhappy relationship, or had no interest in a woman with a young child. None of them had appealed to Merry either. In fact, there had been no relationships that she couldn't happily talk to Dani about because there had been none that were serious!

'If Dani were in love,' she told Zack assuredly, 'then I believe she would have told me about it. And about him!'

'I—' Zack broke off as the sound of the front door opening and closing could clearly be heard.

'That will be Dani now,' Merry warned him softly, putting a lightly restraining hand on his arm. 'Let me handle this, please,' she advised gently as she heard Dani walking down the hallway.

'Mum, I'm home—' Dani broke off her cheerful greeting as she entered the kitchen and saw that her mother wasn't alone, her glance resting interestedly on the man who stood there.

Merry looked at her daughter with pride; she would never cease to be amazed that this gloriously beautiful creature was her own daughter. Almost six feet in height, Dani towered over her. Her hair was a long riot of honey-blonde curls that reached down the length of her spine, and her face as beautiful as any model's, with eyes of deep honey-brown.

Merry glanced sideways at Zack Kingston to see what his reaction was to this vision of loveliness that was her daughter. He looked stunned! But then so did every other man who looked at Dani. Including Zack's nephew, it seemed…

But, seeing Dani now, Merry was even more assured that her surmise concerning that situation was correct; Dani looked as carefree and open as she always did, and if she were hiding something as serious as a secret engagement then she wouldn't have done. Dani had never been any good at keeping secrets!

'Hello, darling.' Merry moved to hug her daughter. 'Had a good day?'

'Pretty good,' Dani responded vaguely, obviously fascinated by the man standing watching them from across the room—which wasn't surprising, considering what conclusion she must have come to concerning Zack's presence here; it was over a year since Merry's last date, and she certainly hadn't brought him home!

'This is Zack,' Merry introduced. 'He just called in for a chat,' she added meaningfully—for his benefit!

'Zack,' Dani greeted, politely shaking the hand he offered before turning to her mother. 'I'll just go and freshen up, and then I'll help you with dinner. Will you be eating with us, Zack?' she added mischievously, obviously intrigued by this male friend of her mother's who had just dropped by for 'a chat'.

Zack looked briefly at Merry. 'Er—no,' he answered huskily. 'As your mother said, I only called in briefly.'

'Oh, well.' Dani shrugged lightly. 'Perhaps I'll see you again some time.' She left the kitchen, her movements unconsciously graceful, taking her boundless energy and effervescence with her, her footsteps soft on the stairs.

Merry gave Zack another glance from beneath lowered lashes. If he had looked stunned before, he now looked speechless!

He swallowed hard.

'She takes after her father,' Merry told him.

'Tall, blond, and gorgeous,' he acknowledged heavily.

Jeff had been all of those things. He had also been a lot of other things Dani wasn't…

'Yes,' Merry confirmed quickly. 'But the important thing is that Dani doesn't look to me like a young girl in the emotional throes of a secret love affair.'

'Or to me either,' Zack rejoined, obviously deeply annoyed now at the embarrassing situation he found himself in.

Which wasn't surprising, really. Zack Kingston gave every impression of being totally self-assured, in control of any situation he should happen to find himself in; Merry could only imagine the inner squirming he was going through at this moment!

'I think I'll take your advice and talk to David again,' he said grimly, putting down his empty wine glass. 'One of us has obviously got his wires crossed.'

As it wasn't Merry or Dani who were at fault, then the blame had to be on his side. Merry felt almost sorry for him. Almost… Except he had put her through some of the most traumatic moments of her life such a short time ago!

CHAPTER THREE

'YOU really should take more care, Merry,' drawled a familiar voice. 'I could have walked off with your handbag just now,' Zack pointed out.

Him again!

And she could see what he meant; her handbag was sitting on the bonnet of the car while she loaded her shopping into the boot.

She straightened. 'I doubt it, Zack,' she told him dryly. 'Mr Patel is a good friend of mine.' She nodded in the direction of the convenience store where she had just done her shopping; the sunny-faced proprietor was undoubtedly watching their exchange through the window. 'And if he failed to stop you, there's five pounds of potatoes in this bag.' She held up a plastic carrier before putting it into the boot with the rest of her bags. 'I would simply have hit you around the head with it!'

Zack's mouth twisted. 'And asked questions later!'

Merry nodded. 'When you regained consciousness, yes.'

He looked at her for several seconds, and then he chuckled, seemingly more relaxed today. 'You would, too!'

'Of course I would; I have all my money in there.' She slammed the boot shut, taking her handbag from his unresisting fingers and placing it inside the car on the passenger seat. 'Wonderful as it is to see you again, Zack,' she said with no sincerity at all, as he made no effort to move away from the driver's door to allow her to get into her car, 'I do have to get on.' She looked up at him challengingly.

To her dismay, he looked just as gorgeous today as he had yesterday, the blue jumper that he wore so casually a perfect match in colour for those 'come-to-bed' eyes of his and he was slim and powerful in black denims.

After he had left her house the previous evening she had convinced herself that he couldn't possibly be as heart-stoppingly handsome as she had thought he was, but, looking at him now, in the rapidly fading daylight, she knew that he was even more so. In fact, he shouldn't be allowed out, was likely to cause traffic accidents. All to women, of course. Because instead of looking at the road they would be unable to take their eyes off Zack Kingston!

She had lain awake in her bed last night thinking about him. And then she'd been furious with herself. To lose sleep at all was bad enough, but to lose it over a man she hardly knew was unforgivable!

'I was just driving over to see you when I saw you come out of the shop,' Zack said, still leaning against the side of her car.

Merry stiffened. 'Why were you coming to see me?' she demanded warily.

'It seems I owe you an apology—'

'Accepted,' she said quickly, knowing exactly what he was apologising for. Casual conversation with Dani over dinner the evening before had assured her that Zack Kingston had definitely made a mistake where Dani and David were concerned.

David Kingston had only come into the conversation briefly, but it had been enough to tell Merry that her daughter had no more interest in him than she did in any of her other new friends at university. Dani certainly didn't know David well enough to realise he had *had* an Uncle Zack, let alone that she was expected to marry into his family!

'If I could just get into my car?' Merry asked pointedly; she was going to physically push him out of the way if he didn't move soon!

Zack gave her a quizzical look. 'Are you usually this rude?'

'With men that accost me in car parks? Yes!'

'So it was true, what you said about the other days of the week!'

She knew exactly what he was referring to. 'You aren't defenceless, Zack—on any day of the week!'

'True,' he responded. 'I would, however, like to make my apology properly—'

'The ground is too wet for you to get down on your knees,' she broke in disparagingly; it had been raining most of the day, adding to the misery of the cold November weather.

He shook his head, his eyes glowing with laughter. 'I had dinner more in mind than grovelling in front of you on my knees!'

Dinner? With this man? He had to be joking! She might as well stand in front of a double-decker bus and simply let it run her down. That was how dangerous she knew this man to be! And she had no intention of standing in front of that bus—or having dinner with Zack Kingston!

'For one thing, Zack,' she sighed, 'I have already accepted your apology—'

'I haven't made it yet,' he put in softly.

'For another—' she glared at him for the interruption '—I have just been into the shop and purchased the makings of dinner for Dani and myself.'

'That's fine,' he said. 'Dani wasn't included in the invitation anyway.'

'And for yet another,' she added with firm determination, 'I have no wish to go out to dinner with you!'

He folded his arms in front of his chest, leaning back against the door she wanted to open so she could get inside the car. 'Tell me,' he prompted lightly, 'have there been many men in your life since Dani's father?'

The question might have been casually put, but the audacity of it made Merry gasp. What on earth did it have to do with him? 'Mind your own damned business!' she responded indignantly.

'Hmm, I thought not,' he answered consideringly. 'Well, I'm thirty-nine years of age, and have never been engaged or married. Although I have no aversion to either state, I just didn't meet the right woman. I own a publishing house, have a home here in London and a villa in the south of France. I like children and dogs, and not necessarily in that order,' he added with a smile. 'Cats tend to make me sneeze, but if you happen to already have a cat, I'm sure I could learn to live with the sneezing. I—'

'Why are you telling me all these things?' Merry finally managed to break in. This man had been an irritation in her life since—was it only yesterday they had met for the first time? It seemed like much longer! Now he wasn't just an irritation to her; he was fast becoming a nuisance!

He shrugged. 'Character reference. I realise all of this is usually covered in the first date, but as you refuse to even *have* that initial ceremony, I thought I should tell you a little about myself.'

'You missed out the bad points,' she taunted. First date, indeed!

He looked sceptical. 'I didn't know I had any,' he mocked.

Her eyes flashed deeply green. 'That arrogance is just one of them! You're also opinionated, judgemental, and—and you're so tall I get a crick in my neck just looking up at you!' she concluded irritably—and then felt irritated with herself. He was too tall…! What on earth was she talking—babbling—about?

It didn't help that Zack's grin widened at her remark. 'If we were seated at a dinner table that wouldn't happen,' he pointed out. 'It also wouldn't apply if we were lying—'

'You're so damned presumptuous!' she cut in huskily, her face fiery red. God, he had her blushing like a schoolgirl! But, considering she had met this man only about twenty-four hours ago, he was being damned familiar!

'On a beach somewhere warm,' he finished smoothly, blue eyes gleaming with laughter—at her expense. 'Don't you find the English winters cold and damp?' he continued, both of them knowing exactly what she had thought he was going to say.

'I love the cold and the damp of England.' She suppressed the shiver that just talking about it gave her. 'I can imagine nothing worse than spending Christmas on a hot beach somewhere.' She shook her head. 'Now, if you don't mind, my peas are defrosting and my chicken needs cooking!'

''I love roast chicken,' Zack told her hopefully.

'I'm deep-frying it.' She had just decided—stubbornly.

He shrugged. 'I can live with that.'

Merry stared at him exasperatedly. She didn't want to invite him to dinner. But as she looked up into his face, the arrogant set of his jaw, the unrelenting steel of his gaze, she had a feeling it wasn't going to be her decision.

Which was ridiculous. She was thirty-seven years old, totally independent; she didn't have to do anything she didn't want to do. And spending any more time in this man's company was not only stupid, it could be downright dangerous!

'Okay, but you're peeling the potatoes,' she heard herself say—her mouth functioning in total opposition to her brain—and then she found herself wondering if he knew *how* to peel potatoes. After all, a man who owned a publishing company, a house in London, *and* a villa in France, was also sure to have that army of servants, like the one she had envisaged serving him breakfast yesterday morning. The breakfast he hadn't been able to eat. Obviously there was nothing wrong with his appetite today! 'On second thoughts, you can lay the table,' she decided—if she had really decided anything at all…!

She had *decided* yesterday that she didn't ever want to talk to this man again. And yet now she appeared to be doing just that…

She also had no interest in having dinner with him, either. And yet now it appeared she was going to… Even if it would be in her own home, and he was going to help her cook it!

Which was precisely what they were doing an hour later, when Dani came into the house. This time her daughter didn't just look surprised to see a man in their kitchen—the same man as yesterday evening!—she looked pleased too!

'Hi, Zack,' she greeted familiarly, bending to kiss Merry lightly on the cheek before helping herself to an apple from the fruit bowl, biting into it hungrily as she sat down on one of the kitchen stools.

'You'll ruin your appetite for dinner,' Merry chided indulgently; she knew from experience that nothing dampened her daughter's love of food, and yet she maintained a model-slim body. Dani could probably eat six apples and manage to eat a full meal afterwards!

Her daughter grinned dismissively. 'This is just to tide me over until my pizza later.'

Pizza? But Dani *had* mentioned something this morning about going out with some friends for a pizza this evening…

Merry had forgotten the conversation during the rush of the day, but it came flooding back to her now. And Zack Kingston had invited himself to dinner. A dinner, it now appeared, they were going to enjoy alone. Enjoy…? It was the last word she should have used to describe the next few hours she was going to have to spend in his company!

'I believe you know my nephew,'' Zack put in conversationally, looking enquiringly at Dani. 'David. David Kingston,' he explained at Dani's blank look.

Dani's eyes widened. 'You're David's uncle?' she looked surprised—but nothing more than that, Merry noted with satisfaction. 'I would never have guessed.' Dani shook her head, grinning widely now. 'You look nothing alike, do you?'

Merry turned accusingly to Zack. When she had asked him yesterday he had told her that he and David had 'a certain similarity'. And she, she remembered now with an inward wince, had said, 'tall, blond, and gorgeous'!

'To look at, no,' Zack replied. 'But in temperament we're very similar,' he amended, with a mocking sideways glance at Merry.

Arrogant, opinionated, and judgemental! Thank goodness Dani *wasn't* heavily involved with the younger Kingston!

'How incredible!' Dani jumped lightly to the floor, almost as tall as Zack in her heeled boots. 'David's coming out for a pizza with us; I can't wait to tell him you're here having dinner with my mother!' She looked pleased at the thought.

'Dani!' Merry panicked at the thought of her daughter leaving her alone here with Zack.

'I'm only going upstairs to change, Mum,' Dani

assured her lightly. 'I'll come back in and say goodbye before I leave.'

'I hope you all have a good time,' Zack put in agreeably, moving so that he stood beside Merry, his arm curving about her shoulders. 'And don't feel you have to hurry back,' he tacked on laughingly.

Merry looked up at him sharply, just in time to see him give Dani a conspiratorial wink. Really! The man had come here yesterday, breathing fire and accusations about her daughter, and now he was giving Dani the impression that the two of them, that he and she, were— There was no 'he and she'!

'Gotcha,' Dani shot back at him before Merry could say anything. 'I'll be down again in about ten minutes,' she warned teasingly, before leaving them alone in the kitchen.

Merry moved pointedly out of the curve of Zack's arm, turning to face him accusingly. 'Exactly what do you think you're doing?' she demanded, green eyes bright with annoyance. 'Dani now thinks— She now has the impression—' Merry could hardly speak!

'Would you rather Dani knows I came here on a wild-goose chase yesterday?' Zack asked. 'That she be made aware of the fact that David made a declaration concerning her of which she has no knowledge? I spoke to David last night,' he added at Merry's questioning look, 'and learnt that he's never so much as taken her out on her own, let alone kissed her or told her he's in love with her! What he was actually saying to me yesterday morning was that he's *seen* the girl he wants to marry, not that he has actually asked her and has been accepted!' he explained.

That was more or less the conclusion Merry had come to—once she'd been able to think at all! And, no, she didn't want to humiliate David Kingston by telling Dani what had happened yesterday. That would only be embarrassing for everyone involved.

Besides, she had done things, made statements herself, at the same age, that hadn't always been tactful or well thought out…

'You told me that David looks like you!' she attacked, not willing to let this man off the hook quite that easily. After all, he was the one who had overreacted…

'No, I didn't,' Zack denied easily. 'I said there was "a certain similarity". And I wasn't referring to the way we look. David is several inches shorter than me, with the dark colouring of his mother. But he's very like I was at his age, over-serious and hard-working—that was the reason I made the jump in assuming his relationship with Dani was an actual thing; David doesn't make light-hearted statements.' He looked rueful. 'He still hasn't. We talked a little about Dani last night, and although the relationship hasn't gone anywhere so far, I can assure you he does intend marrying her!'

'Dani is too young to marry anyone just yet,' Merry insisted stubbornly. 'No matter how serious and hard-working your nephew might be!'

Zack seemed unfazed. 'I would say that's for the two of them to sort out, in their own time. Hopefully, not for several more years yet.' His mouth quirked. 'That's definitely one aspect of mine and David's personalities that differs. Or maybe it's just that I'm older and so there doesn't seem to be so much time; David has immense patience, whereas I—I don't have any patience at all. But then neither of us are children, are we, Merry?' he finished with satisfaction.

She gave him a startled look. *'We..?'*

He nodded. 'David may have taken one look at Dani and decided he wants to marry her, but yesterday I did the same thing where her mother was concerned. That's why, when you asked me, I counted it fortunate that I wasn't already married. You see, there *is* going to be a wedding in the family after all, Merry—ours!'

She had felt this way when she was a child, riding on the merry-go-round, slightly dizzy, slightly disorientated—and very definitely speechless!

CHAPTER FOUR

THE feeling didn't last very long—thank goodness!

'You didn't tell me that insanity ran rife in your family!' she burst out, moving a suitable distance away from him. As much as the confines of her kitchen would allow!

He and his nephew were prime candidates for treatment as far as she was concerned. Dipsticks. Fruit loops. One slice short of a loaf.

However it was put, Zack Kingston was definitely deranged!

He smiled at her now, that slow, lazy smile that only made him appear more handsome. What a pity he was also insane!

'It doesn't,' he answered her easily.

'Then it's just you and David who are afflicted,' she accepted. A day ago she had been quietly living her life, completely unaware of the existence of Zack and David Kingston. And she would like to go back to that unawareness!

Zack shook his head, perfectly relaxed as he leant back against one of the kitchen units, smiling unconcernedly, appearing completely unabashed by the fact that he had just announced his intention of marrying her.

'David and I both have an IQ of over one hundred and fifty,' he drawled mockingly.

'Which just goes to prove the point of that saying "there's a very fine line between genius and insanity"!' Merry cried. 'David appears to be pretty close, but you are obviously way over the edge!'

Zack chuckled softly. 'One of the things I like about you is your sense of humour.'

She shook her head pityingly. 'I wasn't joking.'

'I know that,' he sobered. 'But I wasn't joking either,' he told her seriously.

Completely off his trolley, Merry decided. Thank goodness Dani hadn't gone out yet; she might need some help getting Zack out of the house.

'Mr Kingston—Zack,' she amended soothingly as he raised his brows at the formality; no point in disturbing him unnecessarily! 'How many women have you invited to marry you this week?' she prompted conversationally, willing Dani to finish changing and come back down the stairs. She needed her assistance!

He met her gaze unblinkingly, although there was laughter in the depths of his clear blue eyes. 'I can say with all honesty—'

'Honesty is good,' Merry encouraged, still eyeing him warily.

He gave an inclination of his head. 'I think so too. Dishonesty engenders mistrust, and a relationship cannot be built on either of those things.' He straightened. 'As I told you yesterday, I am thirty-nine years old, and in all that time I have suggested marriage to only one woman. You,' he added, so that there could be no misunderstanding on her part.

Her… Why her? What had she done to deserve being singled out in this way? Or perhaps that was it;

she had made no secret of her feelings towards men and marriage, and maybe Zack Kingston was one of those men who couldn't resist a challenge? Well, he was going to find her a lot more than a challenge!

'I'm sure it's a great honour, Zack,' she told him with heavy sarcasm. 'But my answer has to be no.'

His mouth twisted. 'I haven't asked you yet,' he reminded her.

No, he hadn't asked, but he had told! 'I'm advising you to save your breath,' she bit out impatiently.

'Oh, I don't intend asking you until I'm sure you'll say yes,' he assured her.

'Indeed? Has someone given you prior knowledge of hell freezing over?' she said pleasantly.

Zack chuckled again. 'See what I mean? Great sense of humour.'

'I wasn't joking,' she snapped. 'I'm sure you're a great marital catch, Zack.' If one overlooked the insanity! 'Passably good-looking.' Gorgeous! 'Rich.' The Jaguar XJS that he had driven while he followed her home was testament to that! 'It's just that I've reached the age of thirty-seven without marrying anyone—and I have no immediate plans to change my status!' Dani, where are you? she mentally pleaded with her absent daughter. 'And, in the circumstances, I don't think it would be a good idea for you to stay to dinner,' she finished reasoningly.

'That's a bit unfair—since I helped to cook it,' he protested lightly.

Peeling four potatoes, and two of them for himself, did not constitute helping her cook dinner as far as she was concerned! Although she accepted it was probably the first time Zack had ever peeled even *one* potato—judging by the amount of potato he had cut off with the peel, his hundred and fifty-something IQ obviously served him no useful purpose when it came to practicalities!

'Besides,' he went on persuasively, 'you need someone to help you eat all that food now that Dani is going out.'

Merry's mouth set. 'I don't wish to seem rude, Zack—'

'Of course you do,' he laughed. 'It's another part of your charm.'

Being rude was charming? This man certainly had a warped sense of what he found attractive in a woman. Or perhaps it was just that he was surrounded by yes-men—and women—most of the time…?

'Thank you,' she dismissed. 'I think I'm beginning to understand now why it is you've never married before; you only want to marry women who have no interest in you!' Although, his insanity aside, she didn't think there could be too many of those—besides herself!

He laughed once more, not at all perturbed by her insult. 'That's quite an interesting theory, Merry.' He moved to pour some of the wine from the half-bottle that had been left from the evening before, handing her one of the glasses. 'Completely untrue, of course. But interesting.' He sipped his wine thoughtfully. 'I would just like to repeat that I had never asked *any* woman to marry me before I met you.'

'Then why change the habit of a lifetime?' Merry prompted desperately, taking a thirsty gulp of her wine—a wine, moreover, that was supposed to be sipped and enjoyed, not thrown down the throat like its cheaper imitators. But this man, with his determination, was starting to grate on her nerves.

'You see,' he grinned. 'Life with you will never be boring!'

'I can be boring—if that's what it takes to get rid of you!' she assured him.

Zack folded his arms. 'I'm not going anywhere.' And, as if to prove his point further, he made himself comfortable on one of the kitchen stools.

'I'm thirty-seven—'

'You don't look it,' he assured her admiringly.

'A single mother—'

'We can have more children, if you would like them,' he confirmed softly.

Merry glared at him. He had deliberately misunderstood the statement. 'I spend my days working—'

'Wonderful,' he agreed.

She drew in a breath. 'My nights—'

'We'll get to your *nights* in a moment,' he butted in. 'I'm interested in what sort of work you do.'

'It's completely unnecessary for you to know what work I do—considering we are never going to meet again after tonight!' Merry glared at him.

Zack remained unruffled. 'Humour me,' he encouraged.

She had been humouring him for the last ten minutes; in any other circumstances she would have got as far away from him as possible. But as it was her home he was the one who had to leave. Something he didn't seem inclined to do!

She turned off the heat beneath the potatoes, having no interest in eating them now; a proposal of marriage was sure to rob her of her appetite! 'I teach,' she told him abruptly.

'Subject?'

She sighed. 'Art,' she told him, tensing as she waited for his scorn.

She had heard all the criticism about teaching art, mostly that it was a waste of time—her own and her pupils'. She didn't happen to agree with those critics, felt there was so much more to individuals than their academic capabilities, that there was an artist of some sort inside everyone.

'I should have guessed,' he murmured softly. 'There's a certain style to the way you look and dress,' he explained at her frowning look.

Merry looked down at her long floral skirt and the skimpy black top she wore with it. 'Today's "style" is a charity shop,' she told him dryly. 'And yesterday's was post-Dani; I don't have a lot of spare cash to spend on stylish clothes for myself.' She gave a pointed look at his own expensively tailored clothes.

'I acknowledge the put-down, Merry,' he accepted. 'But I certainly wasn't being patronising—as you thought I was,' he guessed correctly. 'Some people have a style of their own, so much so that they look good in whatever they wear—you are one of those people.'

There wasn't a lot she could say to a remark like that. Fashionable clothes had never been something she was too interested in—just as well, in the circumstances. But over the years she had developed a certain style she considered her own, one that suited the slenderness of her figure and the dark wildness of her long hair. What surprised her was that Zack Kingston had recognised it as such…

Now who was being patronising? Wasn't she giving in to a little reverse snobbery here? Which was totally unlike her. She liked her life the way it was, loved her job, being mother to Dani, and never minded that most people had more money than she did. Even if she had money herself, there was nothing about her life she would want to change. Well… Perhaps one thing. But that was only a dream of hers…

'Thank you,' she accepted huskily.

'Don't be too quick to thank me, Merry,' he replied, blue eyes alight with wicked humour. 'I've also spent a considerable amount of the last twenty-four hours imagining what you would look like *without* the clothes!'

She drew in a shaky breath, colour burning her cheeks as she stared at him wide-eyed. 'You—'

'I'm off now, Mum.' Dani bounced back into the room, lovelier than ever in a brown fitted top and brown jeans that hugged the perfection of her statuesque figure. 'Enjoy your evening.' She grinned at both of them.

'Are you sure you wouldn't like to join us for dinner before you go out?' Merry pressed. 'We—I've cooked plenty,' she amended, annoyed with herself for even verbally coupling herself with Zack Kingston. For goodness' sake, he had been fantasising about her *naked*!

Dani looked puzzled. 'I thought I explained; we're all having pizza.' She gave a hurried glance at her watch. 'I really do have to go now, or I'll be late.'

'Dani?' Zack called to her as she was leaving the room. 'Have you ever been a bridesmaid?' She turned back to him questioningly.

'A bridesmaid?' she repeated. 'No, I—' Her eyes widened as she looked at the two of them, Zack so quietly self-assured, her mother now ashen-faced.

Merry had eyes for no one but Zack, her whole body tense with fury. 'You are taking this joke too damned far!' she bit out forcefully, hands clenched tightly at her sides.

Ordinarily a woman who abhorred violence, she was in danger of hitting him! He had walked into their lives—invaded them!—but he certainly wasn't staying!

'Go ahead and enjoy your evening, Dani.' She spoke as calmly as she could to her daughter, even managing to smile a little. 'Mr Kingston's idea of a joke seems to be vastly different from ours,' she added scornfully.

Dani glanced at him, and then she turned back to Merry—as if she very much doubted he would joke about something like that. 'Sure, Mum,' she said, taking her leave this time without any hindrance.

The silence she left behind her was so heavy with tension it could have been cut with a knife…!

CHAPTER FIVE

'YOU may have helped me prepare the dinner, Zack,' Merry told him flatly. 'But this last fifteen minutes in your company has completely robbed me of any desire to eat!' She turned off the oven—having decided to roast the chicken pieces, after all!

'Love,' he informed her unconcernedly. 'They tell me it does that to you,' he explained at her enquiring look.

Her brow cleared, her exasperation rising. 'Zack, I am not in love. With you or anyone else!' she pronounced firmly. 'I don't even know you. And what I do know I don't particularly like!'

'You've already said that,' he replied. 'For ''arrogance'' I think you should read self-assurance. For ''opinionated'' probably straightforward.' He began to tick off the list of her earlier accusations concerning his nature. '''Judgemental''? No—I don't think so. As for the being tall part, I could just as easily make the observation you're a little on the short side.' He looked at her, a smile playing around his lips.

As well it might. There was certainly nothing wrong with his memory! Even down to that last babbling comment she had made about his height...! Except that it *had* been complete babbling; his height, that air of self-assurance, all combined to make her feel small and feminine. She had battled so hard for years not to feel that way, not to need anyone, to rise and fall on her own merits. And, even if she said so herself, she hadn't done too bad a job of it.

But Zack Kingston, with his smooth self-confidence, made her feel vulnerable, while at the same time his admiration of her independent nature gave her a confidence in that vulnerability. Dangerous territory, indeed…

She couldn't actually be feeling attracted to this man! Could she…?

She glanced across at him, only to find he was staring right back at her. As he saw the confusion in her expression he stood up, moving slowly across the kitchen towards her.

He was going to kiss her, she decided in the split second before he gathered her into his arms and did exactly that!

Insane or not, Zack certainly knew how to kiss, his mouth insistent, and yet at the same time infinitely tender. And then his kiss deepened, passion flaring between them as Zack's arms tightened and his lips became more demanding on hers.

She responded. She would have been lying if she'd tried to claim that she didn't. Her arms up about his neck as she stood on tiptoe to meet him, the curves of her body somehow seeming to fit perfectly into his. Which was odd, given the difference in their heights…

'Mum, could I—? Oops!' gasped a surprised Dani.

Merry broke quickly away from the strength of Zack's arms, though he was reluctant to release her. She moved several feet away from him, turning to look at Dani as she stood wide-eyed in the doorway. Which wasn't surprising; Merry couldn't remember the last date she had been on, let alone when she had last been kissed. And her daughter certainly hadn't been a witness to it!

Merry took a deep breath, her cheeks fiery red. 'Yes, Dani?' Her voice sounded slightly huskier than usual, but at least she had managed to speak!

Flustered as she felt, she hadn't been sure she would be able to speak at all. She still trembled from the intensity of the passion that had risen so quickly between Zack and herself.

Dani looked slightly embarrassed at having interrupted so intimate a situation. 'I forgot earlier. We thought we might all go back to Jane's after our pizza and listen to music. I wondered if I could borrow some of your CDs?' She grimaced her regret at having burst in on them.

'Er—yes, of course you can.' Merry still felt flustered, while Zack, damn him, appeared completely unruffled. Appeared… Because a closer look showed her that his hands, which he was thrusting into his trouser pockets, were shaking a little. Not so unconcerned, after all. 'They're in the lounge,' she told Dani. 'Help yourself.'

'Thanks.' Dani looked relieved at being allowed a quick getaway. Although she paused at the door. 'I promise I won't be back again for hours,' she said mischievously.

'Tactful young lady,' Zack murmured once he and Merry were alone again, the front door closing firmly behind Dani as she left—'for hours'! 'So you like music, too?' he continued, before Merry could make the sharp reply she wanted to. 'David plays music all the time when he's at home,' he explained at her questioning look. 'Consequently I find that my music tastes don't match those of my peers'. He shrugged. 'I suppose that's what happens when you have a teenager constantly about the house.' He certainly wasn't complaining about it, merely making an observation.

Merry hadn't quite looked at it in this way before, but, even though their circumstances were vastly different, Zack was, in effect, a single parent too…

'Not so different, after all, are we?' Zack drawled as he watched the candid emotions flickering across her face.

Her defences were certainly slipping where he was concerned—and it simply wouldn't do!

'Oh, but we are,' she dismissed scathingly. 'No doubt you were able to hire a nanny for David when he was younger—' She broke off as Zack shook his head.

'I felt David had already suffered enough heartache losing his parents at such a young age, and it didn't seem fair that I farmed the responsibility of him out to someone else. So during school terms I fitted my work in around his hours, and during the holidays I worked mainly from home.'

'The benefit of being your own boss?' Merry derided, not letting him off that easily.

'Possibly, Merry,' he accepted harshly. 'Although ten years ago Thorndyke Brooks was a struggling publishing house, and a lot of work was involved in making it viable again.'

Her eyes widened. 'It's Thorndyke Books that you own?'

Now one of the top publishing houses, ten years ago it had been on the brink of bankruptcy. Zack Kingston was the entrepreneur who had stepped in and turned the company around? Very successfully, if she remembered correctly. They had a dozen international top authors working for them now, and their non-fiction books were of a very high standard indeed—several Thorndyke textbooks were used at the school where Merry worked.

'You're *that* Kingston?' His business successes had been reported in the newspapers for years, but somehow she had always imagined—if she had thought of it at all!—that he would be older. Much older…

'It is. And I am,' Zack confirmed. 'And you're changing the subject, Merry,' he added with gentle reproof. 'I was endeavouring to point out the things we do have in common, not the things we don't.'

She knew what he had been doing—which was precisely the reason she had tried—and apparently not succeeded!—in putting him on the defensive for a change. She didn't want to have things in common with Zack; it was so much easier to believe their lives—and consequently the two of them!—were completely incompatible.

'You can't do that, Zack,' she denied, smiling wryly. 'The one doesn't outweigh the other.'

'It would be extremely boring if we were exactly the same, Merry,' he returned dryly. 'It's the differences that add the spark. For instance, I like not knowing what you are going to do or say next.'

She pulled a face. 'I'm going to say something I've already said several times this evening—dinner is off!'

His blue eyes glittered teasingly. 'It's a terrible waste of food, and you don't strike me as a woman who approves of waste,' he responded softly. 'Besides, it's my cook's night off, so you'll be condemning me to a takeaway if you make me leave now.'

'You could always join Dani and David for a pizza,' Merry suggested mockingly.

Zack grimaced. 'The pizza would be fine; it's all those over-intense students I'd find hard to stomach. I can't believe we were ever like that, can you?'

He was doing it again, and it wasn't going to work this time. 'I'm not sure I like being a stand-in for your cook!' She took the plates out of the warmer and began to dish up the food that was rapidly spoiling.

'If you could see Mrs Jenkins you would realise exactly how untrue that remark is!' He grinned, straining water from the peas without being asked. 'I'm quite self-sufficient, Merry,' he stated as she watched his efficient movements. 'I only employed a cook once David came to live with me. Bachelor fare isn't suitable for a growing child.'

She laughed, able to imagine what sort of food he had eaten when he was on his own. 'I'm sure David wouldn't have minded!'

'Maybe not,' Zack accepted. 'But I take my duties as his guardian rather seriously.'

Merry gave him a humorous glance. 'So I noticed yesterday,' she came back.

He grinned again that boyish, heart-stopping grin that was so hard to resist. 'I don't regret yesterday. Oh, I wish I hadn't walked in here with all guns firing and made such an idiot of myself,' he admitted. 'But at the same time, if I hadn't, then I wouldn't have met you.'

There was no answer to that, so Merry didn't make one. 'Would you like to eat here or in the dining room?' The food was served onto the plates now, and needed to be eaten before it got cold.

'Here will be just fine,' he assured her. 'I have a bottle of wine for us in the car. I'll just go and get it.'

A bottle of—? He had intended having dinner with her this evening no matter what!

'Close your mouth, Merry.' He bent and kissed her. 'Find me a corkscrew to open it with, would you?' he instructed, before striding outside to his car.

He couldn't just walk in here and take over! He couldn't— He already had…! She wasn't used to this, had been on her own too long to meekly accept—

Her outraged thoughts came to an abrupt halt as Zack returned to the kitchen and she saw the bottle of wine in his hand. It was exactly the same vintage and from the same region as the one she had given him last night—her favourite wine, a small luxury she allowed herself from time to time. She didn't believe for a moment that it was a coincidence—or indeed a shared taste—that had prompted Zack to choose it; he had clearly made a mental note of it the evening before, and deliberately brought a bottle for them to drink together this evening…

'It's quite chilled from being outside in the car,' Zack told her as he took the corkscrew from her unresisting fingers.

Merry was glad of his concentration on removing the cork from the bottle so that she had time to blink back the tears that were threatening to fall. It had been so long since anyone had cared enough to have noticed such a small detail as the wine she liked to drink. If anyone ever had! Oh, Dani was wonderful, and took a lot of care over birthday and Christmas presents, but Merry doubted that even her daughter had taken the trouble to note what wine she favoured.

But Zack had. And he had noticed her individual style of dressing too…

He was far too observant for comfort. Too much time spent in the company of someone so attentive and she might even start to—No! She was not going to fall in love with Zack Kingston. He wasn't right for her at all. He wasn't just attentive, he took over! He—

'To us.' Zack held out one of the glasses of wine to her, challenge in every muscle of his body as he waited for her to return the toast.

'To Christmas,' she returned dryly, refusing to return such an intimate toast. There wasn't an 'us', and there never would be!

'Just as good,' he nodded his satisfaction. 'Excuse the pun,' he went on, 'but I have the feeling it's going to be a very *Merry* Christmas now that I've met you!'

Merry was quite happy to excuse his pun, it was the quiet determination in his voice that bothered her!

CHAPTER SIX

'TALKING of Christmas—'

'You were; I wasn't,' Merry quipped. The two of them, having enjoyed their meal—and the wine!—were now seated in the sitting room in front of the roaring fire Zack had insisted he build for them in the grate. Merry's reluctance to have him light the fire hadn't stemmed from a need to be independent, but from the fact that she knew it was all too cosy and comfortable with the flames glowing!

Zack looked unconcerned by her interruption. 'I have a pre-Christmas cocktail party I have to attend tomorrow evening. I wondered if you would like to come with me?'

Merry just stared back at him. A cocktail party. Did she look like the type who went to *cocktail parties*?—where dozens of bored people, who usually didn't know each other very well, stood around with drinks in their hands, nibbling away at unrecognisable canapé that did absolutely nothing to satisfy one's hunger. She might have a tiny build, but she had a healthy appetite—as this evening's meal should have told him!—and the thought of spending hours at this man's side, trying to look decorous, did not appeal to her one little bit. Besides—

'I'll take your silence as acceptance—'

'I shouldn't if I were you,' Merry calmly stopped him. 'Cocktail parties aren't my scene.'

'If you're worried about being fed, I promise I'll take you out to dinner later in the evening,' Zack assured her dryly.

She gave him a glare, more because he *had* realised she appreciated her food than anything else. 'You're jumping two steps ahead, Zack, when I've already turned down the original request!'

'Oh, come on,' he cajoled. 'What harm can it do you to come along with me? You'll stop me being bored out of my mind!'

It couldn't do her any harm; she was more than capable of looking after herself! That wasn't the point of her refusal at all. She was an adult, and for the most part she could pick and choose what she did. Accompanying this man to a cocktail party was not high on her list of priorities.

But, a little voice inside her head reasoned, Zack *had* helped her unpack her shopping earlier, *had* helped her to cook dinner, *and* he'd produced a bottle of her favourite wine for them to drink with it. He—

None of those things changed the fact that he had also announced his intention of marrying her!'

In that case, she asked herself almost a day later, as she studied her reflection in the mirror, what on earth was she doing all dressed up as she waited for Zack to arrive before driving them both to the cocktail party?

Merry shook her head dazedly; the man was like

a steamroller, knocking down any obstacles—including the word 'no'!—that got in his way.

She looked at her appearance critically. Not bad, she decided. Not bad at all. The black fitted knee-length pencil-slim dress was almost twenty years old, but it was back in fashion, and considering the amount of times she had found to wear it during those years—nil!—it was in pristine condition. Her figure had returned to its natural slenderness after she had given birth to Dani. Her hair she had left loose in dark curls down her spine, adding a little make-up to her normally peachy complexion and a peach gloss to her lips. Yes, she didn't look bad at all for a thirty-seven-year-old mother…!

She gave a rueful smile as she turned away from the mirror. She didn't look bad, but a thirty-seven-year-old woman, with an eighteen-year-old daughter, was *exactly* what she was—and the sooner Zack realised it the better!

But Dani's comment, when Merry walked down the stairs a few minutes later, did nothing to reassure her she would convince him of that this evening.

'You look gorgeous, Mum!' Dani announced admiringly. 'I don't think I've seen you in that dress before.'

Merry smiled. 'If you had, no doubt you would have borrowed it before now!' Dani was a lot taller than her, but both of them had size ten figures.

Dani touched the silkily soft material. 'It's beautiful, Mom. It must have cost—' She broke off as the doorbell rang.

'That will be Zack,' Merry said gratefully—she

had never thought she would be relieved at his arrival, but on this occasion she most certainly was.

She did not want to get into a discussion with Dani about her dress... Maybe she shouldn't have worn it, but quite honestly she just didn't have anything else suitable to wear. Cinderella in reverse. She did have something to wear to the ball—but that something had already provoked her daughter's curiosity...

Other than telling her she looked beautiful, Zack made no comment on the dress. But Merry somehow doubted its designer-label style had missed his eagle-eyed attention.

She shouldn't have worn it, did not want to pique Zack's interest in her any more than it already was piqued. But the temptation not to look like the poor relation had been too much for her. Vanity. Ridiculous, in the circumstances...

'David and Dani are going to the cinema together this evening,' Zack announced as he drove them to the party.

'I know,' she replied. 'And until a few days ago—' until Zack himself had come into their lives! '—Dani was barely aware of your nephew's existence.' Any more than she had been aware of Zack's! 'Obviously optimism runs in the family!'

Zack grinned unabashedly. 'I told you, David is a lot like me.'

And what David hadn't been able to achieve on his own—Dani noticing him as more than just one of the crowd!—his uncle had done for him. Dani was now intrigued by the Kingston family. David, she had informed Merry earlier, was a very intelligent young man. Dani had never been attracted to overtly good-looking young men, was more interested in the brain behind the looks. Remembering Dani's father, and the way she herself had stupidly fallen for his golden good looks, it was a trait Merry had encouraged in her daughter. David Kingston, Dani had decided, had an 'intelligent' mind…

'I know, I know,' Zack said as he saw Merry's expression. 'I was mad as hell two days ago at the thought of David wanting to marry anyone. But, having now met Dani…'' He paused. 'She's too much like you to be pushed into anything she doesn't want to do.'

'Remember that,' Merry returned quickly, trying to salvage at least some control over what was happening in her own life. This man was a bulldozer, and at the moment she didn't seem to be holding her ground at all. As evidenced by this evening! 'Exactly where is this party?' She changed the subject as she straightened her colourful shawl, its long length covering the dress totally.

'A hotel in the city,' Zack returned economically.

There was something to be said for being driven in the luxury of the XJS, the smell of doe-leather, the warmth of the interior.

The close proximity of Zack in the confines of the sports car…

He looked, and smelt, gorgeous, the black dinner suit and snowy white shirt doing nothing to hide the power of the body beneath, his hair newly washed and gleaming golden, his aftershave elusively male.

No doubt heads would turn—female, of course!—when they reached the party.

Although she was unprepared for the absolute silence that greeted their entry into the crowded private room where the party was being held, or the spontaneous applause that quickly followed that silence.

Merry turned to look behind her, expecting to see someone famous entering behind them. But only Zack and herself stood in the doorway. And as they couldn't be clapping her…

She turned frowningly to Zack as the tiny band at the other end of the room began to play 'For He's a Jolly Good Fellow'. Exactly what sort of party was this? And why was Zack being welcomed in such a fashion?

An elegantly dressed woman in her fifties moved forward out of the crowd to kiss him warmly on the cheek. 'Wonderful party, Zack,' she congratulated throatily.

Merry knew this woman, recognised her instantly. It would be difficult not to; Diana Melbrook was the author of several number one bestselling books, her last having been turned into a television mini-series. The authoress had appeared on several chat shows in the weeks preceding its broadcast.

As Merry glanced around the room she saw several other well-known people: top authors, several actors, a number of television personalities too.

This wasn't just any old cocktail party Zack had

brought her to, this was a Thorndyke Books cocktail party—and Zack, as the owner of the publishing house, was also the host!

What did that make her…?

CHAPTER SEVEN

'YOU'VE stopped smiling,' Zack murmured softly against her ear as the conversation began to flow around them once again and they were no longer the centre of attention.

Stopped smiling? That was the least of her worries! She felt frozen to the spot by what she had just realised, wasn't sure she was going to be able to move when the time came for them to mingle with the other guests.

She had imagined a large, impersonal party, a short time spent in inane conversation with complete strangers, and then the two of them could quietly leave. As the host of this party, Zack could hardly leave until the last guest had gone. Which could be in several hours' time!

She turned to him accusingly. 'You could have warned me!'

He spoke unconcernedly. 'If I had, you wouldn't have come.'

'Of course I wouldn't—' She broke off, breathing deeply to steady her nerves. 'What am I supposed to do now?' Her glittering green gaze told him of her tension.

'Enjoy yourself?'

Enjoy herself...? She didn't know anyone else here, except Zack. No doubt that was what he meant!

She smiled up at him, aware that people were eyeing them curiously. 'I intend getting out of here the first opportunity I get—'

'Merry? Merry Baker? It is you, isn't it?'

Merry froze once more. Not only did someone else at this party know her, and her name, but she knew them too, recognised that voice! It had been about nineteen years since she had last heard it, but it was a voice she would never forget.

'I thought so,' Karen Jacobs drawled derisively as Merry turned slowly to face her. 'You haven't changed a bit.' Her gaze swept over Merry's appearance. 'Same hairstyle. Same dress,' she added pointedly.

Karen obviously hadn't changed, either, she had always been a first-class bitch. Albeit a beautiful one, with an eye for style—which was probably why she'd recognised the dress! It was a talent that had made her editor of one of the top fashion magazines. A tall, willowy blonde, the other woman was as slender as she had always been. Although years ago her hair had been long, now it was cut short, framing the perfect beauty of her face, her eyes deeply blue, and fringed by long, dark lashes.

Merry's eyes turned to the man standing awkwardly at Karen's side; he was tall and dark, almost too good-looking, and there was a weakness about his mouth and in his deep brown eyes that couldn't quite meet Merry's. Here was one person, at least, who would rather not have renewed the acquaintance!

Zack merely looked puzzled by the couple, frowning as he stood slightly on the outside of the group, watching them with narrowed eyes. Like a spectator at a play. Except Merry didn't intend letting him remain that way; he was the one who had brought her here in the first place!

'Darling.' She curved her arm intimately through the crook of his, pulling him gently, but firmly, to her side. 'I would like to introduce you to Karen and Roger Jacobs.'

'Zack and I already know each other,' Karen told her coolly.

Merry nodded. 'But I doubt he realises that you are the younger sister of my sister-in-law,' she said lightly, shooting Zack a warning look as he looked stunned by this information.

As well he might. Karen and Roger Jacobs were as different in lifestyle to Merry as chalk was to cheese; the other couple, with their fine clothes and rich jewellery, were obviously far wealthier than schoolmistress Merry. It hadn't had to be that way, of course, but the price for remaining a part of her family had been far too high for her to pay.

'How *are* Glenda and Stephen?' she prompted Roger, trying to draw him into the conversation; he and Karen hadn't been married when she'd known them all those years ago, but Merry hadn't missed the diamond-studded wedding ring on Karen's left hand. 'And my mother and father, of course,' she added tonelessly.

She couldn't mention Glenda and Stephen without bringing her parents into the picture too. A dutiful son, Stephen, her older brother, had married the woman of their mother's choice. Merry had no reason to doubt that Stephen had since continued to do exactly as he was told. The two of them had been close when they were children, but their differences had become glaring when they were older. 'Dutiful' was not a word that could ever be applied to Merry—or to anything that she did!

Roger didn't look at all happy with this situation. 'They are well,' he answered abruptly, obviously uncomfortable with the whole conversation.

Merry couldn't claim to be exactly thrilled about it herself. As for Zack, he wasn't saying anything, but stood taking in everything that was being discussed. And formulating some questions of his own, no doubt!

'How is your—what did you have, by the way?' Karen raised supercilious brows as she looked at Merry. 'You'll have to excuse us, Zack,' she told him throatily, resting her hand briefly on his arm in a gesture of intimacy. 'As a family, we're always shamelessly lax about keeping in touch with one another.' She gave a tinkling laugh.

Merry returned the other woman's gaze coldly. She hadn't considered this woman part of her family nineteen years ago, and she certainly didn't do so now. Dani was her family now, her only family…

'I have a daughter,' she told the other couple flatly. 'How about you? Do you have children?'

'Certainly not,' Karen dismissed disgustedly. 'I can't imagine anything worse than a screaming little brat hanging onto my ankles. And pregnancy seems to play havoc with a woman's figure,' she concluded bitchily, the fitted red dress she wore showing not an ounce of superfluous flesh on her body.

Zack moved at last, putting his arm possessively about Merry's waist as he drew her closer to his side. 'Let me be the first to assure you that pregnancy did absolutely nothing negative to Merry's body,' he stated, his own eyes challenging now as he looked at Karen. 'She's perfect exactly as she is.'

While she was grateful for his support, at the same time Merry really didn't need the bitchy Karen to get any bitchier—and Zack's remark was sure to make her so!

'Do Glenda and Stephen have children now?' Merry put in quickly.

'No,' the other woman rejoined abruptly. 'Glenda is as averse to pregnancy as I am.'

Merry somehow doubted that; an heir for the Baker family had been paramount in her mother's plans. But it seemed there wasn't one…

'What did happen to that ghastly man you were involved with?' Karen was being deliberately provocative. 'And his equally ghastly wife?' she went on, before Merry could make any reply.

Merry felt herself pale. She hadn't known Jeff was married when she'd fallen so recklessly in love with him. Not that the fact changed anything; he *had* been married, and it had been a marriage he'd had no intention of leaving. Certainly not for a pregnant eighteen-year-old!

She opened her mouth to reply to the insult—only to find Zack had got there first.

'Family reminiscences can be so amusing, can't

they?' he put in lightly, the strength of his arm about Merry not light at all! 'We must remember to invite you all to the wedding.'

'Wedding?' Karen echoed sharply, eyes narrowed maliciously as she looked at the two of them suspiciously.

'Yes—our wedding,' Merry heard herself confirm—and then almost gasped out loud as she realised what she had said.

'Well, well, well,' Karen drawled speculatively. 'Could it be that we hear the patter of tiny feet once again?' she asked, looking Merry up and down.

Merry had moved instinctively to slap the other woman for the deliberate jibe; Karen's implication was unmistakable: Merry would only be able to catch a husband like Zack by becoming pregnant! But again Zack was quicker than her, his hand tightly grasping her arm before it could swing upwards and her hand could make contact with the other woman's mocking, smiling face.

The pleasant expression on Zack's face didn't so much as waver, although only a fool could have missed the steely glint in his eyes. 'Funny you should mention that—' his voice was silkily soft—though that silk barely covered the steel beneath, '—we were talking only yesterday about the possibility of getting ourselves a dog once we're married!'

Karen looked startled, momentarily disconcerted. 'A dog?'

'A dog,' Merry concurred, recovering quickly from the other woman's insults; she was no longer an immature teenager, she was a mother, with a responsible job. She had made a success of her life, she realised, despite her family. 'Cats make Zack sneeze,' she continued conversationally, shooting him a grateful look from beneath lowered lashes; the worst thing she could do would be to reduce herself to Karen's level.

'They most certainly—*atishoo*!' Right on cue, Zack sneezed. 'Please excuse me,' he apologised blandly. 'I—*atishoo*!' He sneezed again. 'It seems it's not only the furry kind that have that effect on me,' he added, his expression one of complete innocence.

Roger shot Karen an apprehensive glance as her face tightened furiously. 'I think we should go and circulate, darling.' He took a firm hold of his wife's arm. 'I'm sure we've monopolised enough of Zack's attention for one evening.'

Karen visibly forced herself to relax, her mouth curving into a fixed smile, although her eyes remained glacially hard. 'It was wonderful to see you again,' she said insincerely. 'Your parents will be pleased to know you've done so well for yourself,' she told Merry haughtily.

Merry replied with stony silence. Her parents, her mother, at least, had shown no interest in her over the last nineteen years, and she had no reason to suppose this chance meeting tonight would change any of that. In fact, she didn't want it to—could imagine nothing worse than having to deal with her mother once again!

'Nice to see you again, Roger.' She moved to kiss him lightly on the cheek, smiling at him reassuringly as he gave her an appeasing look. Roger always had been the nicer of this couple! Although weak, very weak…

'You really are looking wonderful, Merry,' he braved his wife's wrath to tell her warmly.

Not so weak after all, Merry acknowledged lightly, returning his smile.

'I always did like you in that dress,' Karen added as her own parting comment.

Merry gave a rueful shake of her head as she watched the other couple walk away. The rich and the beautiful. How sad they really were.

'Meow,' Zack murmured laughingly in her ear.

Zack!

What on earth must he be thinking of her now? Not only were her family awful, but she was a single mother whose lover had been a married man!

Merry had been so young, not much older than Dani was now. Although she had always loved her father, it had been her mother who'd made the decisions, her mother who had decided on the schools her two children would attend, on the universities they eventually went to. She had even chosen Stephen's wife for him. While Merry's father had been a good man, a kind, loving man, he had always meekly acquiesced to his wife's decisions, aware that she was the one who held the pursestrings.

Merry hadn't realised it at the time—although she had had plenty of time in the years that followed!—but at eighteen she had been looking for a man who was strong and dependable, a man who knew who he was, and where he was going. Jeff had seemed all of those things to Merry's inexperienced eye—but ultimately he had proved he was weaker than her father and brother, a man who used his marriage like a shield while he indulged in numerous affairs that could never go anywhere because he already had a wife! Merry had only learnt the full truth of that when she'd found herself pregnant with his child…

But Zack didn't know any of that, had merely been told by the bitchy Karen that the father of her baby had been a married man. A man who obviously hadn't stood by her when she needed him.

What must Zack be thinking?

He moved to stand in front of her, his hands moving to tenderly cup either side of her face as he tilted it up to his. 'You do realise,' he told her huskily, 'that I intend keeping you to the statement?'

Which statement? There had been so many in the last ten minutes—and none of them complimentary to her!

'The wedding,' Zack explained teasingly as she looked blank. 'I could sue you for breach of contract if you try to back out of marrying me now!'

He could sue her? What did *she* possibly possess that he could sue her for?

Nothing, came the immediate answer. But Zack was telling her, more succinctly than ever, that what he had heard in the last ten minutes hadn't changed how he felt about her at all…!

Merry laughed, a light, relieved laugh. Of course she had no intention of marrying him, but at the same time she didn't want him to think badly of her either. And he didn't…

'That's better.' He spoke his satisfaction at her laugh, his hands leaving her cheeks as he reached down and placed one of her own hands firmly in his. 'And now I believe it's time to get ourselves a drink and circulate.'

'Circulate' meant accompanying Zack as he spoke briefly with every person in the room, Zack charming and assured as he did so. It quickly became obvious that not only did his guests like him, they trusted and respected him too.

Zack Kingston, Merry realised dazedly, *was* a strong, dependable man, a man who knew who he was and where he was going…

Oh, help!

CHAPTER EIGHT

'I WAS eighteen when I met Jeff,' Merry told Zack a couple of hours later, when the two of them were sitting in a quiet restaurant together enjoying a late supper. Although Merry's appetite deserted her the moment she began to talk about that disastrous relationship nineteen years ago. A relationship that had ultimately changed the whole of her life...

She had been eighteen, the daughter of a wealthy family, beginning her art degree. The whole world had been at her feet, her future choices unlimited. Then she'd met Jeff.

'You really don't have to tell me any of this, you know,' Zack assured her. 'I think I know enough about human nature by now to realise that Karen Jacobs is not a nice woman.' He paused. 'That her version of events is coloured by her own unhappiness.'

Merry's eyes widened. 'What makes you say that?' Karen had struck her as a woman comfortable with her own success.

Zack sipped at his wine, his first alcoholic drink of the evening. He had stuck to drinking orange juice throughout the cocktail party, explaining quietly to Merry that it was work and not pleasure. Most of the guest list had been made up of Thorndyke authors, the rest of them television, newspaper, and magazine personalities—hence Karen's invitation at all. Despite the impression Karen had tried to give of a greater intimacy between herself and Zack, Merry knew which version she believed!

'Merry, you have so much more than Karen does. Oh, yes, you do,' he confirmed as she tried to protest. 'Bullies rarely pick on people they actually consider inferior to them, even though it might seem that they do. It's invariably someone who really possesses something they wish they had.'

'I can assure you,' Merry snorted, 'I have nothing Karen could possibly want!'

'How about independence? You obviously broke away from family ties. And personal success—you couldn't look and behave the way you do if you weren't perfectly satisfied with your life exactly as it is— What is it?' he pounced sharply as she pondered this last comment.

'Nothing.' She forced a brightness into her smile. 'None of us can claim to have everything we want.' She excused her brief moment of regret. She had everything she *needed*…

'That's true,' Zack acknowledged slowly. 'I thought my life was running along quite nicely—until I met you and realised it had a damned great hole in it!'

'Zack,' she warned reprovingly.

'Okay, don't believe me,' he said. 'But David is about as close as I've ever had to someone I could sit down and talk to the way I do with you. And as we both know, that isn't the same thing at all!'

She did know. Close as she and Dani were, friends

as well as mother and daughter, that latter relationship precluded her from talking to Dani about some things. Besides, there was a generation gap that wasn't there between Zack and herself.

Help again!

'You're a successful woman in your own right, Merry, through your own endeavours and not through a family connection,' Zack continued determinedly. 'You also have something else that Karen and her sister, your sister-in-law do not have.'

Now Merry was very puzzled. What could she possibly have—Zack? He surely didn't mean himself?

Had that intimate hand on his arm meant something, after all? There was no doubting that Karen was a beautiful woman, and—

'I have no idea what you're thinking now.' Zack cut in on her racing thoughts. 'From the expression on your face, I don't think I want to know, either! I was talking about Dani, Merry,' he explained as she looked at him uncomprehendingly once again. 'You have a child.'

'But—'

'I was watching Roger's face during that part of the conversation.' Zack shook his head. 'Karen may have chosen not to have children; I accept that part of it. But I have a feeling it's something else completely with your sister-in-law. Roger looked taken aback when Karen claimed her sister didn't want children either, which leads me to believe that she probably can't have any... Does that sound feasible to you?' he asked thoughtfully.

Merry remembered her mother's glee when Stephen had married Glenda; her wish had been that the young couple provided her with grandchildren as quickly as possible. And Merry's brother had always been so dutiful…

'How sad,' Merry sighed—and sincerely meant it. Glenda was too much like Karen for her and Merry ever to have been friends, but even so she couldn't help feeling for the other woman, if what Zack suggested was true. It *did* sound feasible.

Her own life would have been so much bleaker without Dani in it. Less complicated too, she accepted that, but she wouldn't change her life for Karen's or Glenda's. Which was exactly what Zack had been talking about all the time…

'Will you see any of your family again?' Zack prompted gently as he watched the emotions flickering across her face.

Merry gave him a startled look. 'Why on earth should I? One chance meeting with the sister of my sister-in-law—the first in nineteen years, I might add—' she told him hurriedly—one step into *his* life and she had been thrown into the company of people she hadn't seen since she was a teenager, whom she'd had no wish to see during that time, either! '—gives me no interest in seeing again the family who totally rejected me and my unborn child!' The last came out slightly bitterly, although it came as a surprise to Merry that she should still feel that way.

She didn't know what reaction she had expected from her parents on learning of her pregnancy, but it certainly hadn't been the one she had got. Of course, her brother, Stephen, weak as usual, hadn't questioned their decision.

'That's what happened, isn't it?' Zack said understandingly. 'You broke the acceptable code, and so they threw you out.' His mouth tightened grimly at the thought.

'Oh, I could have stayed,' Merry informed him with barely concealed distaste. 'All I had to do to remain part of the Baker family was destroy my own child before it was born! It's ironic, really,' she went on. 'That unwanted grandchild is now the only one they have.'

'Their only heir,' he confirmed. 'You didn't tell me you were *that* Baker,' he tacked on playfully, reminding her of her comment when she'd realised he was the Kingston who owned Thorndyke Books.

But she knew exactly what he meant by his remark; the Baker family were old money—owned property all over the world, had shares in numerous companies. Her father had even been the one to change *his* surname when he'd married her mother; as the only Baker heir of her generation, her mother had had no intention of relinquishing hers.

But the name, and all that went with it, had meant nothing to Merry, and she didn't want the family inheritance for Dani either…

'You didn't ask,' she replied. 'And Dani may be the only heir,' she added tightly, 'but she has nothing to do with the family!'

Zack persisted. 'She may not feel that way. And Karen strikes me as a troublemaker…'

He was right, of course; Karen had always liked to

stir things up and then sit back and watch the situation develop! To mention this evening's accidental meeting with Merry to her family would benefit no one. Which was exactly why Karen *would* do such a thing, of course!

'What a mess,' Merry muttered irritably.

'And all my fault,' Zack put in ruefully.

She looked at him sharply, feeling the colour in her cheeks. 'I didn't say that.'

'You didn't have to,' he responded, reaching across the table to take one of her hands in his. 'I can tell exactly what you're thinking. Merry, I'm really sorry this has happened, but at the same time I suggest you let Dani make her own mind up about this if—or when—the time comes. She's your daughter; she'll know the right thing to do.'

Dani *was* her daughter, and she hoped that she had been a good mother to her, that she had instilled all the right values in her. It was just that the Baker family could be so powerful if they chose to be.

Not with her daughter, they couldn't! Dani might only be eighteen, but she had her own code of moral values, a sense of what was right and what was wrong—though a few days ago Merry *had* made the erroneous assumption that Dani was pregnant with David Kingston's child…!

No! Dani was a sensible young lady, would never do anything to hurt someone else, would never be taken in by the lavish lifestyle the Baker family had to offer. Dani simply wasn't impetuous.

Merry wasn't quite so sure about that when they arrived back at the house a short time later and Dani dreamily greeted her at the front door with the words, 'Mum, I've met the man I'm going to marry!'

Not another one! What was *wrong* with everyone all of a sudden?

This was just too much!

CHAPTER NINE

'I *WAS* mistaken.' Zack's voice came from behind Merry. 'David *is* as impatient as I am!'

Merry wasn't in the mood for levity. This whole situation was becoming ridiculous. 'Dani.' She spoke firmly to her daughter. 'I suggest we talk about this once Zack has left.'

'Oh, hi, Zack.' Dani looked at him as he stood in the shadows behind her mother. 'I didn't see you there.' She looked a little embarrassed at having been quite so open in his presence. 'I'll leave the two of you to finish your evening,' she apologised. 'I just wanted to… Night, Mum.' She bent to kiss Merry on the cheek. 'Zack.' She ran up the stairs, not dwelling on her outspokenness.

Merry didn't move. What was wrong with everybody. Had they put something in the water? What, for goodness' sake? Because suddenly everyone around her wanted to get married!

Zack strolled past her into the house, turning back when Merry still didn't move. 'It *was* David she was talking about, wasn't it?' he queried.

Merry shot him an impatient glance. 'Unless she met someone else before or after the film—of course it was David!' She marched determinedly into the house after slamming the door behind her. 'What is it with your family?' she demanded accusingly. 'You have to leave, Zack. You and your nephew. You're turning our lives upside down. We were fine as we were. We don't need—*I* don't need—' Where had these tears come from, cascading hotly down her cheeks, making speech impossible, and her whole body tremble with reaction?

'Merry!' Zack enveloped her in warm, comforting arms, holding her against his chest.

This was exactly what she didn't want! But she was too upset, too tired, too emotionally fraught to fight against it at this moment. She had been fighting too long, alone against so many obstacles. Right now she simply didn't have the strength to fight against the protection Zack's arms gave her against those obstacles. It was all too easy just to give herself up to being the one who was looked after for a change, rather than the one who did the looking after.

She could barely see Zack as she looked up at him through her tears, had no idea how vulnerable she looked. But she did feel the gentle pressure of Zack's lips against hers, the way her body melted into his as she returned his kiss, and not gently at all.

She needed—oh, God, at this moment she needed Zack! To be kissed by him. Not to have to think, if only for a brief time. Bliss!

She had never been kissed like this in her life before!

Zack's lips wreaked havoc on the softness of hers, his arms like steel bands as he moulded her body to the hard contours of his. Once again Merry was amazed at how well their bodies fitted together, even if he was too tall…

She was babbling again—but in her head this time!

Her neck arched as Zack's lips trailed a fiery path to the creamy hollows the black dress left bare, one of his hands lightly caressing the full upthrust of her breast, her nipple pulsating with pleasure beneath the silky material.

'Oh, Zack...!' she groaned weakly, knowing that if this continued much longer she was going to be completely lost. Dani was upstairs—

Dear Lord, Dani! She couldn't behave in this wanton fashion with her daughter only feet away, albeit up the stairs and in her own bedroom with the door firmly closed. Dreaming about David, no doubt!

Zack released Merry reluctantly as she pulled away. 'Don't look so upset, Merry,' he chided. 'It was only a kiss.'

Only a kiss? She didn't think so! The truth of the matter was, she was falling in love with this man. If she wasn't already in love with him! And *that* terrified the life out of her...!

'That isn't what I'm upset about.' She retreated into anger. 'You came here the other day, insisting that my daughter couldn't marry your nephew; now I suggest you go home and tell him the same thing.'

As she warmed to the subject, she really did feel angry. Zack had made things worse by coming here two days ago; until that time Dani hadn't so much as given David a second glance—now it appeared she was in love with him!

'They are both far too young to think about getting married,' she snapped. 'And Dani wouldn't even have thought about taking David seriously if you hadn't piqued her interest,' she accused, eyes brightly green.

'Merry—'

'Don't you "Merry" me in that patronising tone!'

'Another fault to add to the long list?' Zack arched blond brows, his hair falling endearingly onto his forehead.

But Merry only felt more irritated as she noticed his tousled hair—it had been her fingers running through it that had caused the disarray! 'Just the truth,' she bit out coldly. 'You have only complicated my life—'

'Isn't that better than just emotionally skimming along the surface?' he suggested softly.

She became very still. 'Exactly what do you mean by that remark?' But she knew; she *knew*!

Zack drew in a deep breath, slowly releasing it again. 'Merry, I know what you're trying to do—and I'm not going to fight you,' he added quickly as she went to speak. 'I care about you very much, Merry, and I know I've been bulldozing you the last few days. I also accept that it isn't working, that I'm only succeeding in upsetting you. It's my way. See what I want—and go for it. It probably has something to do with that arrogance you once accused me of,' he admitted.

He was trying to lighten up now, and in a way he was succeeding. Because it was his previous remark that had hit her with the force of a sledgehammer. Emotionally skimming on the surface of life... Was that what she had been doing the last nineteen years...?

The first few years after Dani's birth had been hard, looking after a small child, working hard on her degree course, living on a small allowance. By the time Dani began school herself, Merry had been ready to begin her teaching career. Since then, the years had simply flown by, filled with Dani and her job, and her personal life put almost on permanent hold; even the few dates she had accepted had always been with men with whom she had a mutual interest, but whom she hadn't found particular attractive. Emotionally skimming, Zack had called it…

''Merry, you know that I want you in my life.' Zack lightly gripped the tops of her arms. 'But I want you there permanently, as my wife, and I won't accept anything less.'

He was so different from Jeff it was difficult to take in. The last thing Jeff had wanted was to marry her; Zack wouldn't accept anything less…

'I want a white wedding,' he continued with assurance. 'The walking down the aisle and the ''till death us do part'' bits. I would like us to have a child together. But you have to want all those things too. And until you do, perhaps it's better if I stay out of your way,' he concluded heavily. 'I can love and cherish you, but until you love me in return you're only going to view my actions with suspicion—and great caution. I don't want that. I don't want to go on causing you distress, either.'

He was leaving her life! As quickly as he had come into it, he was leaving!

'I'll have a chat with David,' he promised, releasing her, stepping back, the happiness gone from his face now, his expression as grim as the first day he had knocked on her door. 'See what plans he and Dani have. If any,' he added self-disgustedly. 'I won't jump to any conclusions this time!'

And neither would Merry! She had totally misjudged the whole situation last time, although common sense—and her knowledge of Dani—had thankfully kicked into action.

But that was for later, once Zack had gone. Because he *was* leaving. And he wasn't coming back. There was nothing she could do or say that would stop him—because she couldn't say the words he wanted to hear! Maybe it was emotionally skimming, but at least this way no one had been able to hurt her in all these years…

Once Zack was out of her life again, she would be able to return to that.

Wouldn't she…?

CHAPTER TEN

'I KNOW I shouldn't, Mum, but I feel really nervous,' Dani told Merry as they stood outside the huge oak door that fronted the imposing house.

Merry shot her daughter a sympathetic glance. She couldn't claim to be feeling exactly relaxed about this herself. But it wouldn't do for *both* of them to admit to feeling nervous!

Zack had been proved correct in his observation that Karen appeared to him to be a woman who liked to create trouble! He had been right about several other things too, Merry had realised in the week since he'd left her, but those other things she had pushed to the back of her mind, deciding that what they were dealing with now was more important for the moment. After all, tomorrow *was* another day…

Not even a day had passed from the time she had met Karen again to when she'd received a telephone call from her father—she had vowed at that moment to become ex-directory! But the call had to come from her father, of course, because, as they all knew, Merry would have simply replaced the receiver on hearing the sound of her mother's voice. And would have still gone ex-directory!

Her father was another matter completely; Merry had always been close to him during her childhood, and had received no ultimatums from *him* when she'd told her parents of her pregnancy. What her mother hadn't known then, and probably still didn't know, was that her father had visited Merry shortly after she'd given birth to Dani, that he had helped her financially too, during those first few difficult years of studying and being a single mother. It was as much as he'd been able to do when her mother had refused to even have Merry's name mentioned in the house.

She knew her mother had put her father up to the telephone call inviting herself and Dani to dinner; he wouldn't have dared to do it without her mother's consent.

Dinner. Just the four of them, her father had assured her. With no hidden agenda. She had never known her mother *not* to have one, but this time it wasn't so hidden; Dani was the only Baker grandchild, and her grandmother wanted to meet her.

In which case, in total agreement with Zack over this, Merry had felt it was Dani's choice…

Which was the reason they were now standing outside the front door of the Baker residence. Merry hadn't made the same mistake this evening of wearing the classic black dress that had earned her such ridicule from Karen last week! Her dress tonight, newly bought, was the same deep emerald colour of her eyes, and it fitted the tininess of her slender figure perfectly. It might be so in real life, but Merry wouldn't look like the poor relation this evening!

'Your grandfather is wonderful, Dani,' she told her daughter softly. 'My mother—' She stopped, at a loss for words where her mother was concerned—where *any* mother who could reject her own daughter under such circumstances was concerned. She had tried several times during the last week to describe Mrs Baker to Dani, but the truth simply wouldn't do; she owed her mother nothing, but Dani's relationship with her was a completely different matter.

'Don't keep worrying about it, Mum.' Dani squeezed her hand reassuringly. 'I simply want to meet them both. I'm curious, that's all. I don't expect to feel much else,' she added.

Merry's first thought, on seeing her mother again for the first time in nineteen years, was that time hadn't been kind to her. The face that had once been regally beautiful had become pinched and bitter; Eleanor Baker looked all of her sixty-three years!

Merry's father had fared slightly better, tall, and still strikingly handsome in his black dinner suit, wings of grey at his temples in hair otherwise as dark as Merry's own. It was so good to see him again!

'Merry, darling.' He moved forward to hug her. 'You look wonderful,' he told her warmly.

She blinked back the tears, proudly pulling Dani to her side. She *was* so proud of Dani, felt she was the single most perfect thing she had ever done in her life. 'This is my daughter, Dani—short for Daniella.' The last was added slightly defensively as she looked across the room to where her mother stood, looking at them all so aloofly.

The house itself hadn't changed at all since Merry's childhood, still the show-piece of the woman who owned it, the deep red and gold decor somehow seeming to reflect Eleanor Baker's coldness rather than casting the warm effect that it should have.

'Named for your father, of course.' Her mother spoke for the first time since their arrival, a voice well-remembered from the last time Merry and her mother had spoken: cold and slightly condescending.

How her mother must hate having to do this, Merry realised sadly, almost feeling sorry for that. Almost... Too much had been said and done in the past for her ever to completely forgive Eleanor.

Merry's head went back. 'Of course,' she confirmed in a clipped voice, remembering the proud look on her father's face the day he'd realised she had named her daughter after him.

'In that case, my dear,' Eleanor spoke directly to her granddaughter, 'I shall call you Daniella.'

Dani returned her look with unblinking eyes. 'I would rather you didn't. My name is Dani,' she replied clearly.

Merry looked at the two women, the one so much older now, but having lost none of her imperiousness, the other poised on the brink of womanhood—and her expression turned to one of amazement as she saw for the first time that Dani had her grandmother's regal bearing, if none of her snobbery, and a definite will of her own! Her mother, Merry realised with some amusement as she began to relax for the first time in days, had met her match in her granddaughter!

'Very well,' Eleanor accepted after several stunned seconds. 'I'm sure it's a very pretty name.'

'I've always thought so,' Dani agreed.

The initial clash between grandmother and granddaughter, in which Dani had undoubtedly been the winner, set the tone for the rest of the evening, with

Merry's mother avoiding any subjects that might be cause for controversy. Including that of Merry's supposed engagement to Zack Kingston… Karen was sure to have mentioned that little fact to the family as well, Merry was sure. But it was never mentioned.

In fact, the whole evening was more pleasant than Merry could possibly have hoped for. What had seemed to her like a huge mountain to climb had turned out to be nothing more than a small molehill. She would never forgive or forget the way her mother had let her down all those years ago, in fact she might never see her mother again after this evening, but it really didn't matter to her any more. She had faced her mother and felt nothing but a slight sense of pity—for all that her mother could have had, which instead she had so wantonly given up.

'Whew, what a dragon.' Dani's chuckled remark, on their way home shortly after ten o'clock, seemed to echo Merry's thoughts. 'Grandpa is a poppet, though,' she added with real affection, having fallen quite easily into calling him such, while Eleanor had very firmly remained Eleanor!

Merry eyed her daughter ruefully. She needn't have worried on that score either; Dani knew exactly who she was—and wasn't! 'You do realise what tonight was all about, don't you?'

'Of course.' Dani wrinkled her nose inelegantly. 'They wanted to look me over, see if I'm good enough to be a Baker.'

Merry laughed at her daughter's forthright summing up of the evening. Dani was right, of course;

Merry probably just wouldn't have put it quite that bluntly. 'Do you think you passed?' she teased.

'Who cares?' Dani dismissed.

Exactly—who cared any more? That particular Nemesis was well and truly faced as far as Merry was concerned, and Dani wasn't about to let it become one for her.

Dani reached out and squeezed her arm briefly. 'You've been a wonderful mother to me,' she told her huskily. 'The best family anyone could ever wish for.'

Merry swallowed hard. 'Thank you.'

'I'm glad you decided to name me after Grandpa, though. He loves you, and you obviously love him very much.'

'Not as much as I love you,' Merry told her softly.

'What a lucky pair we are,' Dani pronounced with satisfaction. 'And as for my surname; that's going to be totally irrelevant once I'm married to David,' she said happily.

Dani had remained firm in the announcement she had made almost a week ago. Having now met David several times, Merry agreed with Zack that his nephew looked nothing like him, but in other ways he was so like his uncle it brought a lump into her throat just to be in the same room with him.

'Have the two of you decided on a date for the wedding yet?' she probed gently.

Dani shrugged. 'Some time after we've both got our degrees, and before we start medical school.'

Merry had been included in several conversations with the young couple, and she knew that their ultimate aim was to open up a medical practice together—Kingston and Kingston. They seemed to have progressed a long way in a week, but, as Merry knew only too well herself, it *was* possible to fall in love in the space of a second, not to mention in three days…!

'Isn't he sweet,' Dani murmured dreamily at her side. 'I told David how nervous I felt about this evening,' she explained at Merry's questioning look, 'and he's sat here and waited for me to come home.' She pointed to the colourful Mini parked in front of their home.

Merry's own gaze went past the Mini to the Jaguar stationed in front of it. *She* hadn't told Zack she was nervous about seeing her parents again—in fact she hadn't spoken to him for six days—but it looked as if he had guessed her feelings for himself, and decided to follow his nephew's example. He had waited for her to come home, too!

CHAPTER ELEVEN

How Merry's heart ached just at the sight of him!

She had inwardly acknowledged to herself this week how much she was missing him, but face to face with him like this—! She ached, too, to know the warmth of his smile, the deep huskiness of his laugh, the warm strength of his arms, to hear him tell her again that he loved her…

'Zack,' she greeted him tensely, having locked her car door and turned to find him standing on the pavement beside her.

But she had known he was there, had felt him there.

'Mum, David and I are just going for a drive,' Dani called out to her as she got into the car beside David.

Zack looked at Merry closely, searchingly. 'Is everything okay?' he prompted softly as his nephew and Dani drove away.

'Why shouldn't it be?' Merry dismissed flippantly. 'Dani and I have just come back from dinner, that's all.'

His deep blue gaze remained fixed on her face. 'I know where you've been, Merry,' he confirmed gently. 'David told me. I had to come; I feel responsible.'

Responsible? She didn't want him to feel that—it was the last emotion she wanted from him!

She had thought so much about him this last

week—had hardly been able to think about anything else. Thoughts of Zack, and how she felt about him, had even lessened the importance of dinner with her parents this evening. But she had known she had to get that out of the way, for Dani's sake, before she made any move to see Zack.

And now he had come to see her…

What did they do now? If Dani and David had stayed then they could all have gone into the house for coffee, but—

'Invite me in, Merry,' Zack demanded gruffly.

Now that he was here this was all going too fast for her. What if—?

Zack barely waited for the door to close behind them before gathering her up into his arms. 'I've missed you!' he groaned, his face buried in the scented softness of her hair.

She had missed him too. God, how she had missed him. He was deep inside her heart now, and she couldn't seem to get him out. In fact, she had decided in these last days without him that she didn't want to!

'What did you say?' Zack had become very still, raising his head to look down at her with eyes that had gone cobalt blue.

What had she said? She hadn't— She couldn't have—

'I love you, Zack.' The words came out clear and firm this time.

And she was the one who had said them. Not once, but twice!

'You love me…?' He seemed totally astounded by

her admission. *He* was astounded; she didn't even seem to have control over what she said any more!

'Yes,' she confirmed with certainty. 'And there is no responsibility to be felt about this evening by anyone. I realise now that I should have done it years ago.' She shook her head. 'All I can see them as now is two elderly people who have lived their lives by a code, imposed by other people as well as themselves. And because of that they missed out on their granddaughter growing up. I…' She hesitated momentarily. 'I've lived my own life by a certain code these last nineteen years too. It's a code that hasn't allowed people close enough to be able to hurt me. "Emotionally skimming", I think you called it,' she remembered ruefully.'

'Merry—'

'No, let me finish, Zack?' she asked softly. 'Because I've stopped skimming. What's left is a very emotional woman, a woman who wants that white wedding, the walking down the aisle *and* the "till death us do part" bits.' The tears in her eyes blurred her vision, but she knew Zack was still there, could feel him there. 'But only if *you're* the man waiting at the end of that aisle for me. Zack, will you marry me?' Oh, *help*. She quaked inwardly as she heard herself say those last four words.

His arms tightened about her. 'I'll even let you plan the wedding—as long as you make it soon!' he grated.

She didn't care how soon it was. She had been without him this last week—and she had absolutely hated it. She loved this man, every caring inch of him!

'Do you mind if we convert the top of my house into a studio for you *after* we're married? I really don't want to wait until the work is completed—' Zack looked down at her as she gasped. 'I remember you once told me that no one has everything they want, so I asked Dani what it was *you* wanted—and she told me you had always wanted a place of your own where you can paint full time.' He paused and smiled. 'Your wish will be granted, my love.'

Candid, *wonderful* Dani!

'I would like us to have a child of our own, too,' she told him almost shyly. To finally be given the studio she had always wanted would be wonderful, but at the moment she could imagine nothing more exciting than the two of them having a baby of their own to love and care for.

'Remembering your inability to take the pill—I told you I would store that away for future reference!' he joked '—and the way I find it difficult to keep my hands of you, I think that it's highly likely!' he said. 'There's absolutely no reason why you can't paint *and* have our baby, my darling,' he assured her lovingly. 'Together we can do anything!'

Together... It wasn't something she had ever known before. But it sounded and felt wonderful!

And she knew, with Zack, it always would be...

Tender Romance™
6 brand new titles each month
...love affairs
that last a lifetime
Available on subscription every month
from the Reader Service™
GEN/02/RS2